Dinosaur Detectives
Search for the Facts...

Herrerasaurus
and Other
Triassic Dinosaurs

Tracey Kelly

BROWN BEAR BOOKS

Published by Brown Bear Books Ltd

4877 N. Circulo Bujia
Tucson, AZ 85718
USA

and

Leroy House
436 Essex Rd
London N1 3QP
UK

ISBN 978-1-78121-405-3

Library of Congress Cataloging-in-Publication Data available on request

Text: Tracey Kelly
Designer: John Woolford
Design Manager: Keith Davis
Editorial Director: Lindsey Lowe
Children's Publisher: Anne O'Daly
Picture Manager: Sophie Mortimer

Picture Credits
Public Domain: Eva K 4.

Brown Bear Books has made every attempt to contact the copyright holder.
If you have any information please contact: licensing@brownbearbooks.co.uk

Manufactured in the United States of America
CPSIA compliance information: Batch#AG/5609

Websites
The website addresses in this book were valid at the time of going to press. However, it is possible that contents or addresses may change following publication of this book. No responsibility for any such changes can be accepted by the author or the publisher. Readers should be supervised when they access the Internet.

Contents

How Do We Know about Dinosaurs?

Scientists are like detectives.

They look at dinosaur fossils.

Fossils tell us where ancient reptiles lived.

They tell us how big they were.

Great Find
Victorino Herrera was a goat farmer. He lived in Argentina. In 1959, he found a fossil. It was a dinosaur! People named it *Herrerasaurus* after him.

How to Use This Book

This tells you what the animal ate.

🌿 Plant-eater

🦖 Meat-eater

These tell you when the animal lived.

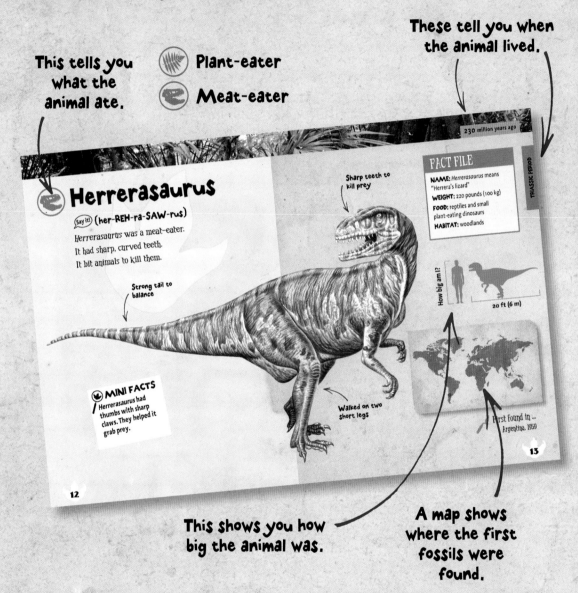

230 million years ago

TRIASSIC PERIOD

Herrerasaurus

(Say it!) (her-REH-ra-SAW-rus)

Herrerasaurus was a meat-eater. It had sharp, curved teeth. It bit animals to kill them.

Sharp teeth to kill prey

Strong tail to balance

FACT FILE

NAME: *Herrerasaurus* means "Herrera's lizard"
WEIGHT: 220 pounds (100 kg)
FOOD: reptiles and small plant-eating dinosaurs
HABITAT: woodlands

How big am I?

20 ft (6 m)

🌿 **MINI FACTS**
Herrerasaurus had thumbs with sharp claws. They helped it grab prey.

Walked on two short legs

First found in ... Argentina, 1959

12

13

This shows you how big the animal was.

A map shows where the first fossils were found.

Read on to become a dinosaur detective!

What Was Earth Like?

Herrerasaurus lived in the Triassic period.

That was 225 million years ago.

Much of Earth was dry desert.

Some places had streams and trees.

Dinosaurs and ancient amphibians lived there.

Coelophysis

 (SEEL-oh-FYE-sis)

Coelophysis was a dinosaur. It ran very fast.
It was a meat-eater. It grabbed prey
with its sharp teeth.

How big am I?

10 ft (3 m)

🔍 MINI FACTS

Coelophysis fossils
were found in New
Mexico. The dinosaurs
had died in a flood.

Long, curvy neck
and long head

FACT FILE

NAME: *Coelophysis* means "hollow form"

WEIGHT: 44 pounds (20 kg)

FOOD: lizards and smaller animals

HABITAT: dry or wet plains

Long tail

First found in ...
New Mexico, 1881

9

Erythrosuchus

(Say it!) (eh-REE-throw-SOO-kus)

Erythrosuchus was an ancient reptile.
It was an ancestor of the dinosaurs
It killed prey with its sharp teeth.

⚘ MINI FACTS

Erythrosuchus's teeth wore out. Then it grew new teeth!

Tail balanced heavy body

How big am I?

16 ft

FACT FILE

NAME: *Erythrosuchus* means "red crocodile"

WEIGHT: 1,000 pounds (454 kg)

FOOD: plant-eating dinosaurs

HABITAT: woodlands

Long, heavy body

Long head, 3 feet (1 m) long

First found in ...
South Africa, 1905

11

Herrerasaurus

 (her-REH-ra-SAW-rus)

Herrerasaurus was a meat-eater.

It had sharp, curved teeth.

It bit animals to kill them.

Strong tail to balance

MINI FACTS

Herrerasaurus had thumbs with sharp claws. They helped it grab prey.

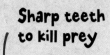

Sharp teeth
to kill prey

FACT FILE

NAME: *Herrerasaurus* means
"Herrera's lizard"

WEIGHT: 220 pounds (100 kg)

FOOD: reptiles and small
plant-eating dinosaurs

HABITAT: woodlands

How big am I?

20 ft (6 m)

Walked on two
short legs

First found in ...
Argentina, 1959

13

Hyperodapedon

Say it! (HIE-per-oh-DAPE-don)

Hyperodapedon was not a dinosaur. It was an early reptile. *Hyperodapedon* had big tusks. It had a beak like a parrot!

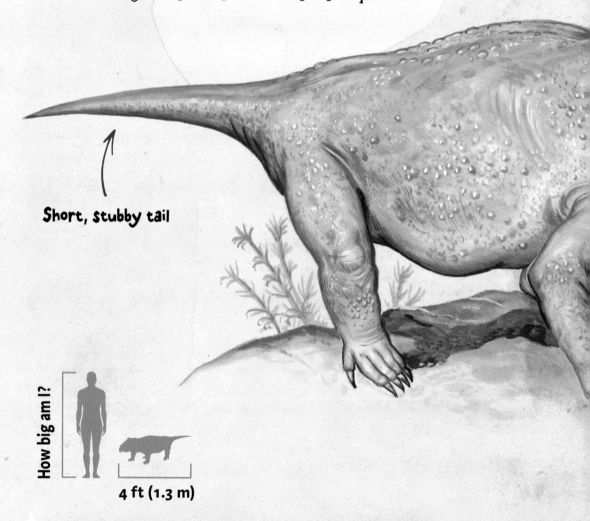

Short, stubby tail

How big am I?

4 ft (1.3 m)

 **MINI FACTS**
Hyperodapedon used its tusks to dig up roots.

FACT FILE

NAME: *Hyperodapedon* means "best pestle tooth"

WEIGHT: 10–20 pounds (4.5–9 kg)

FOOD: seed ferns and roots

HABITAT: woodlands

TRIASSIC PERIOD

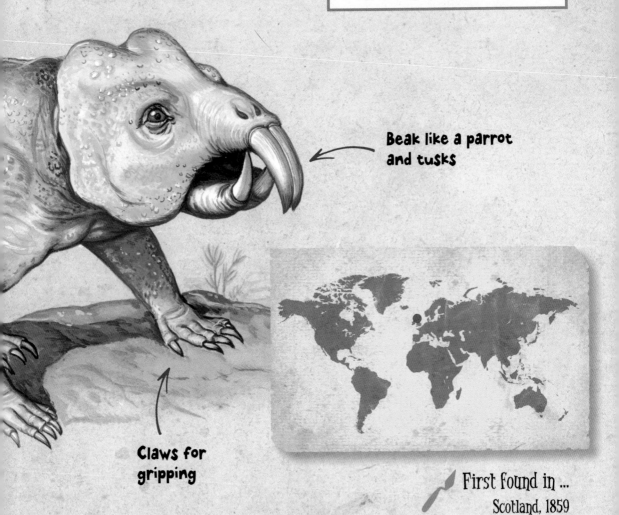

Beak like a parrot and tusks

Claws for gripping

First found in ...
Scotland, 1859

15

Mastodonsaurus

 (MASS-toe-don-SAW-rus)

Mastodonsaurus was a giant amphibian.

It lived in water and on land.

Mastodonsaurus had long fingers.

They helped it grab prey.

 **How big am I?**

20 ft (6 m)

MINI FACTS
Mastodonsaurus was the biggest amphibian ever.

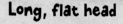

Long, flat head

Bony plates
on back
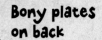

FACT FILE

NAME: *Mastodonsaurus* means
"breast-toothed lizard"

WEIGHT: 440 pounds (220 kg)

FOOD: fish and probably small reptiles

HABITAT: swamps and lakes

Legs for crawling
on land

First found in ...
Germany, 1828

Riojasaurus

Say it! **(REE-oh-ha-SAW-rus)**

Riojasaurus ate leaves from high branches.

Its neck was long and bendy.

Riojasaurus's leg bones were strong.

They held up its huge body.

Long, heavy body

How big am I?

33 ft (10 m)

Small head
and pointed
snout

MINI FACTS

Riojasaurus's thumbs had a claw. It used the claw to fight other dinosaurs.

Long neck

FACT FILE

NAME: *Riojasaurus* means "la Rioja lizard"

WEIGHT: 3 tons (2.7 metric tons)

FOOD: plants and leaves from trees

HABITAT: grasslands and woodlands

First found in ...
Argentina, 1966

19

Tanystropheus

Say it! (TANN-ee-STROW-fee-us)

Tanystropheus was an early reptile. It had a very long neck! It lived near the shore. It snapped up fish to eat.

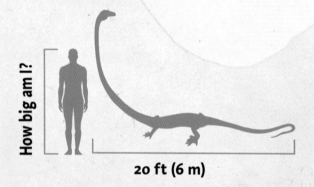

How big am I?

20 ft (6 m)

MINI FACTS

Tanystropheus's neck was longer than its body!

Long tail

TRIASSIC PERIOD

FACT FILE

NAME: *Tanystropheus* means "long vertebrae"

WEIGHT: 300 pounds (150 kg)

FOOD: fish, shellfish, and insects

HABITAT: on the shore by water

Neck had
9 to 13 bones

Long neck,
10 feet (3 m) long

First found in ...
Italy, 1852

21

Dinosaur Quiz

Test your dinosaur detective skills!
Can you answer these questions?
Look in the book for clues.
The answers are on page 24.

 1 Which ancient reptile had a very long neck?

2 What did this dinosaur have on its thumbs?

 3 Which ancient reptile could grow new teeth?

 4 Where were some *Coelophysis* fossils found?

Glossary

ancestor
An animal in the past that
is related to modern animals.

amphibian
An animal that can live in water and
on land, like frogs, toads, and newts.

fossil
Part of an animal or plant in rock.
The animal or plant lived in ancient times.

meat-eater
An animal that eats mostly meat.

plant-eater
An animal that eats only
plants, not meat.

prey
An animal that is
hunted by other
animals for food.

Find out More

Books

The Big Book of Dinosaurs, DK Editors (DK Children, 2015)

Day of the Dinosaurs: Step Into a Spectacular Prehistoric World, Brusatte, Steve, (Wide Eyed Editions, 2016)

Websites

discoverykids.com/category/dinosaurs/

www.newdinosaurs.com

science.nationalgeographic.com/science/photos/triassic-period

Index

Quiz Answers 1. *Tanystropheus's* neck was 10 feet long. **2.** *Herrerasaurus* had claws on its thumbs. **3.** *Erythrosuchus* grew new teeth when the old ones wore out. **4.** *Coelophysis* fossils were found in New Mexico.